MR. SKINNY

by Roger Hargreaves

PSS!
PRICE STERN SLOAN

Mr. Skinny was extraordinarily thin.

Painfully thin.

If he turned sideways, you could hardly see him at all.

And, what made it even worse, was that he lived in a place called Fatland.

Yes, Fatland!

As you can very well imagine, everything and everyone in Fatland was a fat as could be.

Not stout.

Fat!

Fatland dogs were extremely fat!

And you should see a Fatland elephant.

Phew!

And there, in the middle of all this fatness, lived Mr. Skinny.

In the thinnest house you've ever seen.

Poor Mr. Skinny, he didn't like being so different from everything and everybody.

But there wasn't very much he could do about it.

You see, he had hardly any appetite at all.

A Mr. Skinny meal was a very meager affair.

Do you know what he had for breakfast?

One cornflake!

And for lunch?

One baked bean!

And for his snack?

Nothing!

And for supper?

The world's smallest sausage!

And after that, he felt so full he went straight to bed.

In his long thin bed in his long thin bedrooom in his long thin house, in Fatland.

"Oh, I do so wish I could do something about my appetite," he sighed to himself, just before he went to sleep.

"I think," he thought, "that I had better go and see the doctor about it."

And he went to sleep.

The following morning was lovely.

A large fat sun shone down on the fat green trees and the fat yellow flowers, and through them walked Mr. Skinny on his way to see the doctor.

Doctor Plump!

"Come in, come in," he wheezed as Mr. Skinny knocked at his door.

"Sit down, sit down," he wheezed as Mr. Skinny entered.

"And what," he wheezed, putting his plump fingers together, "seems to be the trouble?"

"It's my appetite," explained Mr. Skinny. "I'd like to be able to eat more so that I could put on a little weight."

"Yes, you are rather (how shall I put it) thin," wheezed the doctor, looking at him over his glasses.

"I know," he continued. "let's start the treatment right now!"

He licked his lips.

"This very moment," he added.

And he opened a drawer in his desk and took out an enourmous cream cake.

He put it on the desk in front of him.

And he opened another drawer and took out half a dozen doughnuts.

And put them on the desk in front of him.

And he opened another drawer and took out a dozen raisin buns.

And put them on the desk in front of him,

"Midmorning snack," he explained.

"But it's only ten o'clock," said Mr. Skinny.

"Who's counting?" wheezed Doctor Plump.

And without further ado, he and Mr. Skinny ate the lot.

Mr. Skinny ate a dab of cream, a doughnut crumb and one raisin.

Doctor Plump ate the rest!

"Mmm," wheezed Doctor Plump, popping the last raisin bun into his mouth, and looking at Mr. Skinny.

"I see," he said, "what you mean about your appetite."

He thought for a moment.

"Only one thing for it," he wheezed. "This calls for drastic measures." And he picked up his telephone in his pudgy fingers and dialed a number.

One hundred miles away, the telephone rang.

RING RING! RING RING!

"Hello," said a voice.

Do you know whose voice it was?

"Mr. Greedy speaking," said the voice.

Mr. Greedy listened to what Doctor Plump had to say.

"You'd like a Mr. Skinny to come to visit?" he said.

"To build up his appetite?" he added.

"Delighted," he agreed.

And so, Mr. Skinny went to stay with Mr. Greedy.

He stayed for a month.

And during that time, Mr. Greedy did manage to increase Mr. Skinny's appetite.

And so, at the end of the month, Mr. Skinny returned home.

Happy!

With a tummy!

A tummy was something Mr. Skinny had always wanted.

"I never knew I had it in me," he chuckled to himself.

He was feeling so proud of his tummy, he decided to stop in and see Doctor Plump on his way home.

"I say," wheezed Doctor Plump, looking him up and down.

"Congratulations!"

"Tell you what," he went on. "This calls for a celebration!"

And he opened his desk drawer.